Rule and Camryn 3: The Wedding

B. Love

Soar young girl. Soar.

www.authorblove.com

This is a work of fiction. Names, characters, places and incidents either are products of the author's imagination or are used fictitiously. Any resemblance to actual events or locales or persons, living or dead, is entirely coincidental.

For information about bulk purchases, please contact B. Love via email – authorblove@gmail.com

Previously in Rule and Camryn 2

Camryn had been home all of eleven days before Rule was calling her and telling her that he had to have her for at least one night alone. She stood firm as she promised her Mother she would but folded when Rule told her he'd take her back to Vegas.

A weekend trip didn't count as shacking up, right?

On their way to the airport Camryn thought back over her life and how far she'd come.

Her Father was present in her life and her relationships with her siblings grew stronger day by day.

Her Mother and Father agreed to give love a second chance once his divorce was finalized, and since Victoria wasn't putting up a fight Edward figured that could be happening within thirty to forty five days.

Rule hadn't gone into full detail about what he did to Maurice, but he guaranteed her that she would never have to worry about him anymore. In fact, Leonard seemed to be a man of his word because when Rule went back to his home the next day, Leonard was packing up his belongings. He told Rule that when Maurice was released from the hospital they were moving back to St. Louis.

It was finally time for Elle to leave Memphis for California to start her choreography position for So You Think You Can Dance. Power's attitude had been horrible since Elle announced that she'd be leaving soon, but she promised they'd do whatever it took to make her time away from him quick and stress free.

He'd already started looking into properties to rent on the weekends when he didn't have to teach at Kirby.

Camryn was in her own world as she looked out of the window until Rule passed the airport. She looked over at him and smiled at the sight of his.

"Where you taking me?" She asked.

"You'll see," he said before cutting the radio up.

Camryn rolled her eyes and shook her head as she returned her attention to the window.

Fifteen minutes later Rule was pulling up to empty acres of land.

"Where we at?" Camryn asked.

"Alexander and Goodman."

"In Olive Branch?"

"Yep."

Rule got out and went to open Camryn's door.

"Rule…"

"Do you trust me?"

"You know I do."

"Then step out of the car."

Camryn put her hand inside of his and did as she was told.

"How many acres is this? Whose land is this? This would be the best place for a barn and a garden. I don't see any houses for miles so whoever owns this could build their dream home from scratch."

"It's 3.73 acres. That's what I was thinking when I drove by this place a couple of days ago. It's enough land to build a couple of houses out here. Is that something you'd want to do?"

Camryn looked at him skeptically before turning around and taking in all of the free and open land around her.

"I'd love for us to build our home, baby. That would be awesome. And we can have a barn with lots of animals?"

"Absolutely."

"And gardens?"

"Whatever you want."

"Yay! Then we have to buy some land like this. I know you're not going to let me, but I can afford to go half on it with you."

"You don't have to. I already bought this."

Her smile fell as she turned to face him.

"Wh-what did you say?"

"I said I bought this. This is our land. I rode by here a couple of days ago when I was coming back from the car auction. You remember I was telling you that I was looking for some new additions at the lot?"

"Yes…"

"Well, I drove by it and I thought… damn… this is a lot of land. I could build my baby a home that we can raise our kids in, and she'll still have enough space for her animals and all that fresh food she's going to grow."

"No! No! No! No!" Camryn squealed as she jumped up and down.

Rule smiled and took a step back.

"You didn't warn me! You didn't tell me to get off my birth control," she whined with tears flooding her eyes.

"That's what makes this a surprise," he mumbled as he pulled a ring box from his pocket.

"Rulleee."

Rule put his pointing finger over her lips and silenced her, then he wiped the tears that started to stream from her eyes.

He tried to get on one knee but Camryn grabbed him and stopped him.

"Oh my God," she whispered.

"Woman, will you let me do this?"

"I'm scared."

He chuckled before kissing her sweetly.

"Don't be."

His face turned serious as he took her hand into his and kneeled before her.

"When I met you, Cam, I wanted you, then I couldn't stand your ass. But that only made me want you even more. Day after day that we spent together in Vegas allowed me to pull back the layers of your heart and see you for who you really are – a beautiful, stubborn, strong, submissive, crazy, corny, smart, and passionate sweetheart.

You accepted me in ways no one has before and I knew the day we had lunch at The Top of the World that I would spend the rest of my life chasing you to give you mine if I had to. Thankfully it didn't take that long… but I promise I would have. So… I said all of that to say… I dan bought this land and it needs to filled. You gone marry me and give me some babies now or what?"

Camryn ran her fingers over the freckles on his nose and cheeks before jumping into his arms – causing them both to fall.

"Is that a yes?" Rule asked through his laugh as she saturated his face with kisses.

"Yes, yes, yes!"

Six Months Later

Camryn's day had been long. She met with Brenda and Braille for their fifth wedding dress trip. Still unsuccessful. Unsuccessful and fed up. Why had it been so hard to find a dress? A dress to marry the man she loved just as much if not more than she loved herself. A dress shouldn't hold this much weight... but it did. Without the perfect dress, Camryn refused to have the ceremony her mother and father wanted for her. Without the dress she would sneak away with Rule to elope.

To say their vows in front of a Justice of the Peace and be done with it. As she stared at her red eyes in the mirror that idea didn't sound half bad.

With Elle being in California now, she offered to fly Camryn out to Los Angeles to look for a dress and she happily agreed. Power was traveling with his old student, who was now a member of the Memphis Grizzlies basketball team, so four to five days out of the week and weekend he was gone, leaving Elle bored and open for company.

Elle had even gone as far as to try to fly Grace from San Francisco to Los Angeles, but every time she reached out to Grace she would tell her that she was at work, or at school, and couldn't leave.

Grace and Braille were the same age. Both Juniors in high school. Camryn and Elle tried to keep eyes on the growing girls, but understood at the same time that there were things in life that they would have to experience to understand.

After Camryn's shower she put on the button down shirt Rule had earlier and made her way to their bed. She tossed half of her body over his and he squeezed her tenderly.

"Now why you put my shirt on? You know that makes me want to get inside of you," Rule complained as he pushed her curls out of his face.

"Baby, not right now. I'm tired."

"I know you are. That's why you need to take this off."

"If I take it off that'll only make it worse."

"True. So I take it you didn't find a dress that you liked at all today?"

Camryn lifted her head from his chest and looked into his eyes. Hers filled with tears. Rule closed his and inhaled deeply before lifting himself slightly and kissing her forehead.

"You will find the perfect dress, baby. Don't stress yourself out."

"But what if I don't?"

"You will."

"But what if I don't?"

"You will."

"But what i-"

"Cam, you will."

She nodded and placed her head back on his chest.

"Are you hungry? Did you talk to Power today?"

"I could eat. I talked to him."

"He still doesn't know if he'll be able to come to the wedding?" Rule shrugged and remained quiet. "This is just fucked up. We can't have a wedding without a dress and your brother, Rule. We'll just have to go to the courthouse and take care of this shit." She lifted herself and looked into his eyes again. "The wedding isn't what's important, right? It's about what we invest in our marriage."

Rule smiled softly. "Who you tryna convince? You or me?"

Her smile matched his. "Me."

"You will find a dress, Camryn. With your picky ass. That's the problem. You're too damn picky. And difficult."

Camryn slapped his chest before running her fingers over his cross brand.

"How you gone talk about me while I'm going through?"

"Your ass ain't going through. I bet half the shit you tried on was dope. You need to just let me pick your dress."

"I am not letting you pick my dress."

"Why? You don't trust me? I got style."

"You might dress well for a man but I'm not trusting you with my wedding dress, Rule."

"Ain't it for me, though?" He licked his lips and stared into her eyes until she looked away.

"Yea, I guess."

"So I should know what I want to see you in, right?"

"Right."

"Then let me choose. I promise you'll love it."

"It better not be red," she mumbled giving in.

"Mane, see…"

"See! I'm not about to play with your crazy ass! You gone have me up there looking crazy in a red dress!"

"Nah. I'll have you looking like the dope sexy woman that you are. Fuck tradition. We doing this shit our way. If I want you in a red dress you better believe that red dress gone be bad as hell and you gone be off the Richter scale classy and beautiful in it."

Her cheeks raised as she blushed and ran her fingers across the freckles on his.

"Okay, let's make a deal."

"What's the deal?"

"I'll go in one store in Cali with Elle, and if I don't find anything there you can pick it."

"Cool. Just make sure you leave your measurements here because I know your choosy ass ain't gone find nothing."

Rule pushed her off of him softly and rolled out of the bed.

"Where you going?"

"To fix me something to eat."

"I'll fix it."

"I can do it. I know you've had a long day."

"I want to."

Rule stopped walking and looked back at her. She was in the middle of the bed with her legs open wide enough for him to look at the glistening between her legs.

"My favorite meal," he mumbled as he walked back over to the bed and crawled between her legs.

I know you.

The next day, Rule took Camryn to Andrew Michael Italian Kitchen for dinner. She learned that he liked tucked away places where he wouldn't run into anyone he knew. When he was with her... all he wanted was her.

He was also a fan of this restaurant because of its décor. With its wooden floors and tables and home style design that's exactly how Rule felt – as if he was right at home. They both had the beef and broccoli entrees, and although Camryn insisted that she didn't want any dessert he ordered her the chocolate sticky toffee pudding and the mascarpone cheesecake for himself.

After taking a bite of her pudding Camryn's eyes landed on his cheesecake. She placed her elbows on the table, her face in her palms, and stared from his face to the cheesecake. Rule groaned and shook his head as he took another bite. He refused to allow her to bully him out of his dessert with her pouty lips and puppy dog eyes.

"Don't ask me for none of my stuff, Camryn," he muttered before taking another bite.

"I'm not," she spoke softly.

"Stop looking at it."

Camryn turned to her right partially for a second before returning her gaze to his cheesecake.

"You don't even like cheesecake. That's why I specifically got this one," Rule continued.

"Well... that looks good, though."

Rule sat back in his seat and stared at her in disbelief.

"So you not gone eat the pudding?"

"I told you I didn't want it."

"You always say that then you end up eating all my stuff."

"Well... I told you I didn't want it."

Camryn smiled at the sight of Rule's flaring nostrils.

"Baby, you need to work on your temper," she observed as she slid her hand across the table towards his plate.

"Don't touch that plate, Camryn."

"Let me taste it, baby, please."

"No. We have to go through this shit every time we go out."

"Well..."

"Well nothing. You don't even like cheesecake. You just want it cause it's mine."

Her widening smile confirmed that to be true.

"Just let me taste it."

With a shake of his head, Rule put a bite of cheesecake on his fork and held it to her mouth. Camryn happily accepted and twisted her face up immediately.

"Ew. I don't see how you eat that. It tastes like... ew. Like... clotty milk."

"Camryn, that don't even make sense."

"Yes it does. That's disgusting."

"Good. Now I know what to order."

She rolled her eyes and took another bite of her pudding. Rule opened his mouth to speak but quickly closed it. Power was heavy on his mind. He wanted to tell her that he talked to Power and that he wouldn't be able to make it to their wedding after all, but she was already stressing over her dress. He didn't want to deepen her load. It was his job to remove it.

"What's wrong?" She sensed the change in his energy.

"Nothing."

"We lying to each other now? What's up?"

She pushed her plate further into the table and scooted closer to him.

"I talked to Power."

"What did he say?"

"That when we get married it'll be during the playoffs and one of the stipulations of the contract that he signed to be Wesley's personal coach was that he attend all playoff games. He's been trying to find a way around it but he can't."

He lowered his head to avoid her seeing the sadness in his eyes. Rule and Power had shared every monumental moment in their lives together. This would be the first Power would miss. And because he was used to always being able to count on his big brother, Rule didn't know how to feel or react.

Camryn took his hand into hers and brought it to her lips. She kissed it softly and placed it in her lap.

"We can push the date back, Rule."

"Nah. We already have the invitations. The venue. It'll be okay. I'll get up with him when he has time."

Rule looked at her and smiled to reassure her but she frowned softly.

"Rule, I know you," she said simply.

His smile fell. He let out a hard breath and sat back in his seat.

"I want him to be there, but that's just not possible. As long as I have you I have all I need."

He removed his hand from her lap and retrieved his wallet. Camryn stood and waited for him to place a couple of bills on the table to cover their food. Rule stood and she wrapped her arm around his waist. At that moment, no words needed to be said. At that moment, he knew that she knew what he needed most – to be inside of her, where the worries and cares of this world were overshadowed by the overwhelmingly pleasurable waves of her ever flowing river.

Does Rule know?

Rule was right, but Camryn was in no rush to call him and tell him that. She still didn't find a dress in Los Angeles with Elle. After spending all of their morning and afternoon hopping from store to store they went to grab some hot wings and settled back into Elle's temporary home.

"Sooo…" Camryn cooed. "Catch me up. What's been going on? I'm surprised you haven't gone crazy from not having Power around you every day."

"Girl, I'm on the verge." Elle smiled, but Camryn knew she was serious. "I miss him so much, Cam. Like… to go from spending every day with him to this… I don't know how much longer I can do this."

"Four months. That's how long you have to do this. Four months."

Elle sighed and scratched her nose.

"I just miss him. We're doing what we have to do. He comes here whenever he can and I go to him as much as I can… but it ain't nothing like being in your home with your man."

"I feel you. What's up with Grace? She still avoiding you?"

"Well, she texts me. She keeps telling me the second she has some free time she'll come visit, but I don't know. I'm tempted to go to San Francisco and pop up on her. If I knew where she worked I would. Has Braille said anything about her? I know they were cool before Grace left."

"Nah. She said they haven't been talking since she left. She said they shoot each other a text every once in a while but that's it. She's always at school and work she says. Have you talked to her parents?"

"Nope. Her father doesn't want to talk to me and of course her mother is going right along with it."

"That's just crazy."

"Speaking of father's what's going on with yours and aunty Brenda?"

"You know his divorce was finalized. They're dating. Taking it slow."

"That's good. Layla and Lonnie good?"

"Yep. We're all good. Well… Rule isn't. He's feeling some type of way about Power not being able to come to the wedding. I told him that we could push it back but he wants to go forth."

"I wish there was something we could do. I've looked over his contract to try and find a loop hole but I can't. I sent it to their Lawyer so I'm waiting to hear back from him. I hate this."

Camryn smiled softly and scrunched her curls.

"There's uh… something I need to tell you, Elle."

Elle swallowed hard and crossed her legs.

"What? Not something else bad…"

"No. No. Something… good. Really good."

"Well, what? Spit it out."

"I… I'm pregnant."

"What?!" Elle jumped from her seat and grabbed Camryn's shoulders.

Camryn laughed and sat Elle back down.

"How? I mean I know how, but I thought you were on birth control?"

"I was. I got off a month ago. He's been harassing me about having his babies so… I got off."

Elle's eyes watered as she covered her mouth with her hands. Camryn looked away as hers watered as well.

"You mean… I got a little baby in here?" Her hand rested on Camryn's stomach.

Camryn nodded and wiped tears from her cheeks.

"Yep. It's a baby in there."

"Congratulations, boo! Does Rule know?"

"Not yet. I've been trying to find the right time to tell him, but it never falls out of my mouth."

"This is so great. This. This is just. Just. So great. So so…"

"Elle! Snap out of it."

"Sorry. I just can't believe this. We have to go shopping."

"We don't even know what I'm having yet."

"We'll just get yellow and white stuff until we find out."

Elle took one last bite of her hot wing and grabbed Camryn's hand, lifting her from her seat.

"Fine, but we have to store it here until I tell Rule."

"That's fine. Ahhh I can't believe it! I'm going to be a GodMama!"

It's the least I could do.

On one of the few off days that Power had he went to Los Angeles to spend time with Elle, then stopped home to check in with Rule. He watched as Rule looked over the tuxedo selections and shook his head.

"Ion wanna wear no tux," Rule whined.

"Then don't."

Rule looked back at Power and smiled.

"Camryn would have a fit if she walked down that aisle and saw me in what I really want to wear."

"What you wanna wear?"

"Mane, Ion know. Not no standard black tux, though."

"You want something that suits you? That's understandable. I can't see you in no black tux either."

Power stood and walked through the rows and rows of tuxedos and suits. He returned to Rule holding a white dinner jacket with black and gold lapels and pocket trimmings. Instead of keeping the black and gold pocket square the jacket came with, Power pulled it out and replaced it with a red one. The same shade of red the slacks he'd chosen were.

Power handed Rule the jacket and pants and went rummaging through the aisles again. This time when he returned it was with a white button down shirt with black buttons, and a black bow tie.

"This shit is fly as fuck," Rule mumbled taking the shirt and tie from Power's hands.

Power smiled softly and sat back down. "It's the least I could do."

Rule nodded. "It's cool. I know you'd be here if you could."

Power nodded.

The brothers looked at each other briefly before Rule went back to the dressing room to try on what he knew would be the winning attire.

It's perfect.

Camryn's eyes lit up as she walked around the new home she would soon be sharing with Rule. Right after he proposed they started their search for an architect who could draw up their dream home. With the blueprint in hand Rule hired the same team who built his parents' home years ago.

The kitchen was pale blue in color. In the center of it was a pale blue island with thin legs and brass lanterns hanging above it for lighting.

The walls were covered with a blue fish scale backsplash.

Instead of a traditional sink they installed white marble twin Whitehouse Collection Fireclay Sinks facing each other on the edge of the island.

The living room was empty except for Rule's baby grand piano and guitar. He'd had a wooden bookshelf built into the walls along with a fireplace on the opposing side.

Their breakfast nook had built in shelves and a beautiful glass view of their land.

All of the flooring downstairs was wooden. So was the ceiling. And along with their Den the laundry room and guest bathroom were downstairs as well.

Their upstairs was carpeted a deep cream color. Camryn had no preference for their four bedrooms upstairs. Her only request was that they have a separate Jacuzzi tub and walk in shower with his and hers sinks. Rule willingly gave her what she asked for. Their extra rooms had yet to be decorated, but they knew one would be for Braille when she visited.

As Camryn stood in the middle of the smallest room she fought the urge to tell Rule about the growing baby in her womb.

"You ready to see the barn?" Rule asked pulling her from her thoughts.

She looked at him and blinked tears from her eyes. His expression fell as he walked towards her.

"What's wrong?" His hands cupped her cheeks.

Camryn smiled as more tears fell. She covered his wrists with her hands.

"Nothing's wrong. This is just… beautiful. I'm just a little overwhelmed."

Rule looked down at her as if he didn't believe her, so she stood on her tip toes and kissed him gently.

"I'm fine, Rule."

"You sure?"

"I'm positive. I love you."

"I love you."

"Show me my barn."

Rule grabbed her hand and led her to their backyard. She gasped at the sight of the traditional red barn with a timber frame porch and custom braces. Without waiting to go look inside she jumped into his arms.

"Thank you, thank you, thank you! I'm so excited!"

"You ain't even looked inside yet, crazy."

"I don't have to. It's perfect. Rule?"

"Yea, baby?"

"I... I'm..." She closed her mouth as her eyebrows wrinkled.

"You're what?"

"I'm... hot. Can we just go?"

"You don't want to look inside?"

"No. It'll make me want to stay here now and I know it's not ready yet. Plus, we still have to get the furniture in. I'll wait until we move in to look inside."

Rule looked at her skeptically as she ran her hands down the back of her neck.

"Fine," he agreed.

She smiled and hugged him again. Rule grabbed a handful of her hair and lifted her head from his chest. He looked into her eyes as if he could find what she was hiding from him. When he couldn't find anything he released her and they went back to the house to lock up and head home.

That's what you are.

Rule hadn't told anyone that he applied to Grad school. He wasn't sure if he'd get in. Sure, he graduated at the top of his class… but there was that part of him that's inside of us all. That part that doubts. So to avoid having to mask his disappoint in front of those he loved he kept it to himself until he received an answer.

To celebrate he took Camryn to Ruth's Chris steakhouse. When she declined a glass of wine Rule looked at her as if she was a stranger. She smiled and lowered her head.

"What's up with you? Since when don't you drink?" Rule questioned.

"I just want water tonight. No big deal. Honestly, I'm ready to go. I told you about wearing your glasses. Wine will just make me want you more."

"Umhm," he mumbled disbelievingly.

They ate for the most part in silence. He ordered a T-bone steak while she indulged in a petite filet. For dessert Rule ordered a piece of white chocolate bread pudding and placed it in the middle of the both of them.

"What do you want?" Camryn asked with a smile as he handed her a fork.

"Why I gotta want something?"

"You never share your dessert with me."

"I can't share with my wife?"

Her shoulders caved. Her smile fell. Her eyes lowered.

"Rule…"

"That's what you are."

"Yea, but… I've never heard you say it before. It sounded so good."

Rule blushed and took a bite of the pudding.

"I'm scared to eat this. I need to know what it's going to cost me," she continued putting the fork down.

Rule chuckled and shook his head.

"It's not going to cost you anything, baby. I'm just in a really good mood. I have some good news actually."

"What?"

"I um… you remember when I said I'd consider going back to school?"

"Yep."

"Well, I applied for graduate school."

"You did? Why didn't you tell me? That's great, baby! What are you going for?"

"I didn't say I got in. Maybe I didn't and that led to something else."

She looked at him skeptically before taking a bite of the pudding.

"No. I know you got in. There's no way you could not get in. You're the smartest and wisest man I know. So what are you going to study?"

Rule ran his hand over his face to hide the fact that he was blushing.

"Counseling."

"That's great, Rule. I'm so proud of you."

"You are?"

She nodded with a smile before pulling his face to hers for a kiss.

Camryn broke their kiss. "You're going for your Doctorate?"

"Yep. You need to go for yours too."

"So that means I'll be calling you Doctor Owens?"

"You'll be calling me Daddy before you call me Doctor... but eventually yea."

Camryn rolled her eyes and took another bite.

"I'm so proud of you, though. For real. I knew you were going to go back. Just in your own time."

"I appreciate you staying on me yet not pressuring me."

"That's what I'm here for."

"Yea, well... now that that's out the way I'm over sharing."

Rule pulled the plate in front of him.

"Really, Rule? You gone tease me with it then take it away?"

"You getting a little too comfortable. I said we could share it not you could have it."

She rolled her eyes again and stole another bite.

"Just order another one," she ordered with a mouth full of food.

"Nah. When I order two you don't eat it."

"Ima eat this one."

He looked her over briefly and shook his head.

"You just be bound and determined to do the opposite of whatever I say, huh?"

Camryn shrugged and kissed his cheek.

"You love me for it, though."

"I do. I really do."

Back together again.

The wedding was two days away and they had just finished their last rehearsal. Both of their families filled the reception hall and ate and talked amongst themselves.

Camryn was deep in her conversation with Rule until Edward walked over to her and asked to speak with her. She stood and followed him over to an empty corner.

"What's wrong?" She asked.

Edward smiled and shook his head. His fingers entangled with hers.

"Nothing's wrong, honey. I just… you know that your mother and I have been dating again."

"Right."

"I was wondering if you'd give me your blessing to ask her to marry me."

Camryn clutched his forearm with one hand and her heart with the other.

"Are you… are you serious?"

"I am."

"That's… I… yea… sure… of course… go for it." Edward chuckled then kissed her cheek. "Just… promise me that you'll be good to her. She deserves nothing but the best."

"I agree. That's all I plan to give her, honey. I give you my word."

"Okay. When are you going to propose?"

"Now. While all of her family is here. I want her to see that I'm not afraid or ashamed of my union with her."

Camryn smiled and fanned her face.

"Go before she gets suspicious of me being all emotional."

"Okay. Thanks, honey. I love you."

"I love you too."

Camryn returned to her seat next to Rule.

"What was that about?" Rule questioned.

"He's going to propose."

"Word? Right now?"

"Yep."

She grabbed Rule's hand and watched as Edward walked over to Brenda. They couldn't hear what Edward was saying as he held Brenda's hand and looked into her eyes lovingly. But it must have been something good and sweet because Brenda was blushing and covering her face.

Slowly Edward kneeled in front of Brenda and Brenda stood with shock covering her face. Camryn squealed and resisted the urge to run over to them. Edward pulled a ring box from his pocket and Brenda searched the room for Camryn.

Camryn stood and waved and nodded. Brenda pointed down at Edward like she couldn't believe what he was doing. Camryn chuckled and blew her a kiss before sitting back down in her chair sideways.

Rule wrapped his arms around her from behind and kissed her cheek.

"I love you," he whispered into her ear.

"I love you." She kissed his cheek.

"Yes!" Camryn heard Brenda yell.

She returned her eyes to her mother and father and watched as Edward pulled Brenda into his arms. The shuddering of Brenda's body brought tears to Camryn's eyes. Finally, her family was back together.

I want my brother here.

The day had come. Rule and Camryn were moments away from exchanging vows. Elle made her way to Rule's room to grab Camryn's dress. Neither of them knew what he'd picked, and they both were anxiously waiting to see.

When Elle made it to his room she couldn't help but notice the saddened look that covered his face. He looked up and tried to smile when he saw that it was her, but she'd already seen him in his true mellow state.

On what was supposed to be the happiest day of his life Rule looked withdrawn and unenthused. Ignoring the peach fitted dress covering her body, Elle kneeled and placed her hand on Rule's thigh.

"What's wrong? You're not having second thoughts about this are you?"

"Of course not. I just… I'm nervous. And I want my brother here."

Elle smiled softly at the same time that tears threatened to pour from her eyes.

"I want your brother here too."

"Her dress is hanging up on the door. Tell her I can't wait to see her in it."

"Is there anything I can do? Say? Bring you?"

Rule shook his head and covered her hand with his.

"Nah. I 'preciate you, though. I'll be fine when I see her coming to me, Elle."

Elle stood and cupped his face with the palm of her hand. She caressed his cheek with her thumb softly. His hand covered her wrist and he closed his eyes. As if he was trying to pull some of her calm into him.

"I'm gonna go get her ready for you, okay?"

Rule nodded and released her. Instead of returning to Camryn's room Elle stood between both in the hallway and called Power.

"Legs…" He spoke.

"Can you call your brother? He's in there looking all sad and helpless. I feel so bad."

"I'll do better than that. I'll be there in about thirty minutes. Can you stall the wedding until I get there?"

"Really? Baby… how'd you…"

"I'll explain everything when I get there. I'm on my way. I love you."

"I love you too. You're the fucking best, Power."

Power chuckled and Elle sped walked to Camryn's room.

"I'll see you in a few, Legs."

"Okay."

Elle disconnected the call and smiled so hard Camryn stood nervously.

"What's got you all happy?" She asked as she pulled the dress from Elle's hand.

"I just talked to Power. He's on his way. He said he'll be here in about thirty minutes. Do you mind waiting?"

"Of course not. Does Rule know?"

"No. He looked so down and out that I called Power to see if he could call Rule when I left his room. That's when he told me that he was on his way."

"Thank you Jesus! Okay. This is what I need you to do…"

Just process it.

Per Camryn's instructions Elle went back to Rule's room and blindfolded him with a piece of black cloth she'd found in the choir room of the church.

Camryn walked inside and smiled at the sight of Rule seated in basketball shorts and a t-shirt. His hands were cupped in his lap as he circled his thumbs around each other. She stood before him and traced his freckles gently. Rule jumped, but quickly calmed himself at the recognition of her touch.

Her fingers went from his cheeks to his neck. Then she pulled his shirt from his body and rested the palm of her left hand on the branded cross in the center of his chest. His hand covered hers and they held them there until the beating of his heart slowed down.

"Did you like the dress?" He asked.

"I haven't looked yet. I wanted to come in here and check on you."

His arms wrapped around her body and he pulled her into him.

"I'm good, baby. I'm better now that you're here. Even though I can't see you."

She smiled and ran her hands down his face before kissing his lips sweetly.

"Not until I'm walking down the aisle."

"I know I know."

"Listen, I have something… two things to tell you."

"Go for it."

"First, Power is on his way here."

Rule's grip around her waist tightened.

"Really?"

"Really. He wants us to wait about thirty minutes for him to get here."

"Please? Can we please?"

She smiled and rested her forehead on his.

"Absolutely."

Rule released a long breath and kissed her chin.

"What's the second thing?"

"Ummm…" Camryn pulled her head from his. "I… um… God this is hard."

"What is it, baby?"

"I got off of my birth control a little over a month ago."

Rule's arms fell from her waist. He tried to remove the blindfold but she grabbed his hands.

"No, Rule. You can't see me."

"Mane, fuck that," he mumbled pulling at the blindfold again.

"Rule! Keep this blindfold on! And stop cursing in this church."

"I have to see you, Camryn. Are you saying what I think you're saying?"

His hands went from his face to hers. The feel of her tears had tears falling from his. Camryn climbed onto his lap and kissed his tears away.

"Say it, Camryn. I need to hear you say it, baby. Say it. Say it."

"Okay. I… I'm pregnant."

For seconds on end he sat there in silence. With his head nestled in the middle of her chest. With her running her hands up and down his back.

"You're pregnant? My baby is having my baby?"

"Yes, baby. Your baby is having your baby."

He smiled and exposed those dimples she'd fallen in love with the first time she saw him.

"Really, Camryn?"

"Really."

"About time." Rule wrapped one arm around her waist and put his free hand over her stomach. "I… can't… I don't know… Camryn…"

Camryn chuckled and pecked his lips.

"Just process it. We'll talk after the wedding."

Rule nodded and kissed her again.

"Thank you, Cam. I love you so fucking much."

"What I say?"

"I'm sorry. You got me in my feelings. Just go."

"How you gone put me out when I came down here to see about you?"

"I'm ready now. My nigga on his way. I got a baby inside of you. I'm 'bout to levitate out this damn church."

"Rule!"

"I'm sorry. I'm sorry, God. He knows my heart."

Camryn rolled her eyes and stood.

"I'll see you in a little while, Rule."

"That you will. I love you, girl."

"I love you too."

"Give me one more kiss."

Her smile made it difficult. He smiled and made it impossible.

"Just go. Go and get ready for me, baby," he said softly pushing her away.

"Okay."

Camryn kissed his forehead and left the room excitedly.

Power

Light taps from a knuckle on the door gained Camryn and Elle's attention. They looked at each other and smiled. Power. Elle stood and inhaled deeply.

"Go see your man, boo."

"I'll be right back."

Camryn nodded and straightened up to finish getting her hair flat ironed. Elle stepped out of the room and into Power's arms.

"I'm so happy you're here," she whispered into his chest.

"Me too, baby. Me too. I couldn't miss this. I'm tired of missing you."

She pulled her chest from him and looked into his eyes.

"What does that mean?"

"I can't do this anymore, Elle. I need you. I need my wife. My priorities need to be realigned. I need to be with you starting our family instead of living my NBA dream through Wesley."

"Power, you don't have to…"

"I have a replacement there now. Depending on how Wesley performs with him I may be able to get out of my contract. I went to Wesley man to man and told him he needed to play tonight like his life depended on it because mine does. I'm coming back to you."

Elle pulled his face down to hers and kissed him deeply. Power absently wrapped her legs around his waist and pushed her into the wall.

"Power… we can't."

"You're right. I'm sorry."

Elle waited for him to release her and put her on her feet but he didn't. She chuckled softly and ran her hands down his chest.

"Let me down, baby."

"Not yet."

"Rule has something very important to tell you."

"It can wait."

"No it can't. Besides, if you don't leave now we're going to end up making love right here."

"That's fine with me."

"Power, go."

"Fine."

Power placed her on her feet and pulled her dress down.

"Are you going back to L.A. with me tomorrow?" Elle asked.

"I am. We need to get started on making a baby."

Elle's cheeks were flushed as she pushed him away.

"Go talk to your brother."

"Okay. I'll see you in a few minutes. I love you."

"I love you too. Thank you for coming… and for making that decision. I would have never asked you to and I would have done whatever it took to make it work, but, Power, I can't tell you how happy I am right now."

"You don't have to tell me. Just show me tonight."

Stones

The aisle of the church was covered with red roses and sunflower petals. Lit candles sat at the end of each pew. Their white cushions along with the white marble flooring, walls, and ceiling created an ambiance of holiness, love, and purity that those inside of the room knew would encompass Rule and Camryn's union.

Rule rocked back and forth as he waited for his bride. Power looked over at him and chuckled before grabbing his forearm and keeping him still. Rule nodded his thanks and took a deep breath as their cousin began to sing Stone by Alessia Cara.

"So much on my mind. I think I think too much. Read between these lines. Unspoken way of words. Time comes to rest when you are by my side it blurs…"

Camryn stood at the doors of the church and snatched Rule's heart from his body. His breath from his lungs. His sight from his eyes. They blurred with tears as he watched her begin her slow saunter to him.

Rule chose a custom made red heart shaped backless lace vintage dress with an A-line train. The top of the dress was sheer and showed most of her skin minus the lace flowers that were perfectly placed to cover her breasts, the middle of her stomach, and parts of her sides. The bottom of the dress was sheer with a high and wide slit that showed off her left leg.

As much as she hated to admit it, Rule had picked the perfect dress.

He flung his head back. As if that would stop the tears from falling. When it didn't he tried to walk towards her but Power stopped him.

"Let her come to you," Power whispered.

Rule looked over at Power and shook his head.

"Don't you go into King Manner in this church."

Rule rolled his eyes and nodded. A few steps later Rule sighed and groaned.

"Camryn!" Rule yelled, causing the singing and piano playing to stop. "Hurry up!"

Camryn laughed and wiped her tears as she nodded.

"And I will follow where this takes me. And my tomorrow's long for the unknown. When all is shaking be my safety. In a world uncertain say you'll be my stone…"

By the time she and Edward were halfway down the aisle Rule lost all patience. Quicker than Power could grab him, Rule left his side and walked towards Camryn. She shook her head and smiled as she cried even harder. Rule took her face into his hands and kissed her tears away.

"Why you taking so long, baby?" He whispered into her ear.

"I'm walking at the same pace I walked in rehearsal, Rule."

"It's too slow. It's taking too long. I need you now."

Camryn wiped his tears and nodded.

"I'm here. I'm here."

With Edward on one side and Rule on the other she walked the rest of the way with a bright smile on her face.

"Nothing's sure but surely as we stand. I promise I will stay the same. And I've never seen forever, but I know we'll remain…"

Finally, they stood in front of the Pastor who had a satisfied smile on his face surprisingly.

"That's a first," Pastor Brown mumbled.

Rule looked at Camryn and smiled.

"I understand that you two want to avoid the traditional and exchange rings and stones alone? And your vows?"

"Yes sir," they replied in unison.

"Okay. Son, turn towards your bride."

Rule slowly turned sideways and faced Camryn who immediately hung her head. Rule lifted it by her chin.

"The stones," Pastor Brown continued.

Rule turned to receive his from Power.

"As you hand them to each other I want you to tell one another what these stones mean to you. Rule, you go first."

"This stone represents what I want to be for you. The man that keeps you grounded, safe, and steady. The man that you can always count on no matter what."

Rule kissed the stone then handed it to her. She held it in her hand for a few seconds before putting it in the box Pastor Brown held. Then, she turned around and took hers from Elle.

"This stone represents what I want to be for you. The woman that keeps you focused. The woman that gives you strength. The woman that you can rest and rely on."

Camryn kissed the stone and handed it to him. He held it briefly and kissed it before putting it in the box.

"Your vows. Rule."

Rule took both of her hands into his and smiled at the worried look on her face.

"Ima do right," he assured her softly. She smiled and nodded. "I had this long paper full of promises that I wanted to make. Half of which I'd probably struggle to keep. All of the things about you that I loved. Some things I can't stand. But the truth of the matter is I can't put into words how full my heart is because of you. What I feel for you goes beyond love. Beyond happiness. It's like… you literally are me. You're that in tune with me. I don't know what I did to deserve you, but I thank God for you. And I vow to spend the rest of my life showing you just how grateful I am to have you in my life."

"Rule…" she moaned with tears filling her eyes. "That was beautiful."

He nodded and looked away from her to avoid getting emotional again himself, but when she spoke again he looked at her.

"I don't think I'm the most emotional woman. Well, I am now." She chuckled thinking about how much the baby had her crying lately. "But I've never really been into expressing myself and talking about myself. You pulled me out of myself when I was in a dark space emotionally. You pulled my guards down and exposed my heart, my soul, myself to me.

You've taught me that my memories have nothing on my reality. My present with you. You are my present. My gift from God. You've taken my scars and turned them into beauty marks.

And now that I'm loving and truly living… there's no way that I could do this without you. So, you're stuck with me for life, dude. And I vow to make it as loving, crazy, and passionate as you've made mine."

She wiped the tear that was sliding down his cheek.

"Let's exchange rings," Pastor Brown said looking at Power and Elle who were wiping tears of their own.

Elle handed the ring to Camryn. Power handed the ring to Rule.

"Camryn," Rule paused as he slid the ring onto her finger. "I give you this ring as a symbol of my love. As it encircles your finger, may it remind you always that you are surrounded by my loyal, unconditional, and enduring love."

"I will forever wear this ring as a sign of my commitment and desire of my heart."

"You better."

Camryn giggled and slid the ring on his finger.

"Rule, I give you this ring as a symbol of my love. As it encircles your finger, may it remind you always that you are surrounded by my loyal, unconditional, and enduring love."

"I will forever wear this ring as a sign of my commitment and desire of my heart."

"Well, by the power vested in me by the state of Tennessee I now pronounce you husband and wife. You may now kiss the bride."

Rule shook his head and picked Camryn up. He tossed her over his shoulder and carried her down the aisle.

Camryn laughed and looked from Elle, to Braille, to her mother. She waved at them all before wrapping her arms around Rule's waist as best as she could.

"Rule, you bet not drop me."

"Mane, ain't nobody gone drop your little ass."

"Rule!"

"I'm sorry!"

Epilogue – For real this time!?!

Rule had been fascinated with the thought of what their children would look like since before she was pregnant. The idea of a person being half of him and half of her consistently flew over his head. The idea of there being a piece of him inside of her growing. His literal seed. Giving birth to a child. Caused him to shake his head every time he thought about it.

Now, he sat next to her holding their son, Reign, with a heart filled with fear and love. Reign was the perfect mix of them with his gray eyes, dimples, and freckled cheeks. Rule ran his nose over Reign's cheek and kissed it softly.

Afterwards he stood and handed him back to Camryn.

"You going to get everybody?" She asked.

"Yea. Braille and Elle been out there pacing so long Power sent them away. They just made it back."

"Has she eaten yet?"

"I think that's where they went. Ever since she got pregnant you know Power been on her ass about eating and resting."

"I'll be glad when she has him. Reign and their baby will be able to grow up together like we did. Like you and Power did."

"Yea, well… don't think that's gone get you out of giving me another baby."

"Whatever, nigga. I ain't going there with you. This one ain't even an hour old and you talking about another one already?"

"Hell yea. Soon as I get permission from your Doctor I'm going back in and planting some more seeds."

"Boy, bye. You gone wait at least a year."

"Pah. That's what you think."

"That's what I know."

"Mane, whatever."

"Just go get my folks with your inconsiderate ass."

"Yea, yea. You just hold my son up like the Prince he is."

Camryn rolled her eyes and smiled. There was no point in arguing with Rule. There were just some things he allowed her to get away with and some things he didn't. Giving him more babies was one thing she knew she would never be able to argue or talk herself out of.

THE END? – okay... one more!

CPSIA information can be obtained
at www.ICGtesting.com
Printed in the USA
LVOW01s0251190417
531316LV00008B/177/P